LOVE AT THE ANTIQUES SHOW

Thirteen Tales of Yesteryear

LOVE AT THE ANTIQUES SHOW

Thirteen Tales of Yesteryear

By

Robert M. Turner

iUniverse, Inc.
New York   Bloomington

Love At the Antiques Show
Thirteen Tales of Yesteryear

iUniverse books may be ordered through booksellers or by contacting:

iUniverse
1663 Liberty Drive
Bloomington, IN 47403
www.iuniverse.com
1-800-Authors (1-800-288-4677)

Because of the dynamic nature of the Internet, any Web addresses or links contained in this book may have changed since publication and may no longer be valid. The views expressed in this work are solely those of the author and do not necessarily reflect the views of the publisher, and the publisher hereby disclaims any responsibility for them.

ISBN: 978-1-4401-4806-4 (sc)
ISBN: 978-1-4401-4808-8 (hc)
ISBN: 978-1-4401-4807-1 (ebook)

Printed in the United States of America

iUniverse rev. date: 6/5/2009

This book is lovingly dedicated to the memory of my parents and grandparents who told me most of these stories.

Clara Corine and Orbin Marion Turner
Eunice Ella and Gilbert Dooley Henslee
Maude Belle and Albert Ambrose Turner

Contents

Holy Smoking Gun

The booth at the antiques show was crammed with western memorabilia and was of much interest to many of the men who walked by. A couple of old saddles under the table, some worn, unusually fancy boots, a few rodeo award belt buckles, hand-made spurs and even a shelf of Zane Grey novels all contributed to the uniqueness of the display. However, no item in the booth attracted more comment and interest than the six-shooter pistol housed in the glass case. It wasn't that the pistol itself was so unusual; rather it was the carved ivory handle that drew the attention. A cross had been crudely carved on the handle, and the initials JWF were underneath it. People had fun joking about the incongruity of a cross on a pistol, and there were countless speculative remarks as to what those letters may have meant.

No one realized that the last time the gun had been fired was at a camp meeting revival in West Texas in 1914. The initials were those of the evangelist John Wesley Foote. In fact, that camp meeting and that gun were involved with the demise of his ecclesiastical career. He was well known in that part of the country for his fiery preaching and horse-trading ability. For several years, he had traded horses all winter and held revivals during the summer months under those quickly made brush arbors and tabernacles.

A bevy of churlish cowboys had taken great delight in tormenting the evangelist, chiefly because he attacked their lifestyle and habits. In a community not far away, the cowboys had slipped a rope around one of the supports of the tabernacle and had pulled the loose structure down on the congregation.

Similar actions were anticipated at this revival, but Brother Foote was prepared for them. As the service began, he simple laid the pistol on the right hand side of the pulpit and when the cowboys began their antics, he waved his pistol in the air and announced that there would be no aggravation from them in his services. The marauders knew that the preacher was dead serious and that he was a good shot. The gun rested on the side of the pulpit for the next two evenings, and the revival was free from harassment, at least from the cowboys.

Cousins, Orville and Oran, ages 9 and 8, found the camp meeting the highlight of their year. They were much impressed with the pistol and it gave them new bravado. Most of the farm families came by wagon for the evening services. Babies were plentiful and slept in the wagons close by during the services. Mothers could always tell if a crying baby were hers and would go to see about her offspring. The children and babies slept all the way back to their homes each evening. On the third night of the revival, Oran and Orville slipped out of the preaching and in the shadows crept around to where the wagons were hitched. There they exchanged the babies from wagon to wagon, making sure that each wagon that had held a baby still had one, just not the one they brought.

Of course, it was dark when the meeting broke up. The wagons sleepily rolled to the homes which were miles apart. Most families did not discover their fresh editions until they reached their homes. What few telephones there were in those modest farmhouses were constantly in use far into the night hours. There was nothing else to do but to take care of someone else's baby until the situation could be straightened out the next evening. Reunions and examinations and sagas were abundant on the next night! Never did it become known who had played the trick, but suspicious eyes were cast on Orville and Oran.

The boys thought it best to become faithful attendees of the children's Bible story class which was taught by Miss Brearley, a retired missionary. Their attention wandered a great deal. On a five-minute break from class, the boys visited the outdoor privy, which inspired yet more trouble. The temporary outhouse had been erected on the side of the hill. Of course, it was a two-seater because ladies then felt better about going to the outhouse in pairs. The boys noticed the knot holes underneath the seats in the back of the privy.

Needless to say, the boys were somewhat elated about their success in the baby exchange. Even greater satisfaction came from getting by with the prank. As Orville pointed out those two knot holes in the back of the structure, he pondered, "Oran, can you imagine what might happen if someone howled like a wolf through those holes when someone were in the privy?"

"Not me," said Oran. "That's just too close to the action."

"Well," answered Orville, "What if a bird were pushed through those holes? That should stir up a hornet's nest." They agreed, but an afternoon's effort failed to produce a bird of any size. The idea of the willow branches first tickled across Orville's mind.

"What if," puzzled Orville, "we very quietly stuck some long willow branches through those holes and wiggled them around a bit just to tickle?" Now that was a plan with potential! The red hair and freckles, of which they both had plenty, fairly gleamed as they proceeded with their intrigue.

Little did they anticipate that the first two attendees

would be their mothers. Once the ladies were seated the boys quietly stuck the branches through the knot holes and twirled them around. Oran and Orville had anticipated some screams and mad people, but what they did not anticipate was that both women jumped up at the same time and the makeshift toilet tilted forward falling on the hillside, making it impossible for the women to push open the door. There were plenty of screams, but no one was close enough to hear except two boys. Orville and Oran, after quickly assessing the situation, suddenly vanished into thin air. They were not about to either help upright the privy or call anyone else to help, on the grounds that it would certainly incriminate them.

The ladies existed in that uncompromising position for about half an hour until someone else came up the hill. According to them, their travail had been a much longer time. Oran's mother even claimed she had been bitten. Thankfully, she did not show the scar.

"There was some sort of wild animal under there that snapped and made the most hideous scream," Oran's mother panted.

"I've never been so terrified in all my life," Orville's mother chimed in, as someone offered her some smelling salts. "I just think I am too disturbed to go to the preaching tonight. This camp meeting is finished anyway if more safety can't be provided for us women," she vowed.

There was shock and awe on many faces as the women elaborated their experience. A few of the men snickered and slight grins were seen often on most faces for the rest of the day. However, no one dared to laugh openly. From then on, women went to the privy in groups of three and Oran and Orville became more attentive than ever in Miss Brearley's Bible class for the children.

As a matter of fact, they even became interested in what she was teaching. In order to grasp the attention of the children, she had developed lessons on stories about snakes in the Bible. The children's favorite, of course, was that of Moses who threw his staff to the ground and it wiggled. There were five passages in Isaiah alone about snakes. Orville and Oran loved all of them. Revelation boasted some stories about serpents, which Miss Brearley emphasized and even told them about religions which employed snakes in their worship.

It did not take Oran and Orville long to make the decision that they wanted to belong to the religion that danced with snakes. They began early to plan for their witness on the final night of the revival. It was then that people sat on the mourner's bench and made confessions and affirmations about their faith and religious experiences. No one seemed to notice that Orville sat on the outside seat on one side of the tabernacle and Oran sat on the other side. Both had a burlap sack near their feet. When Brother Foote urged more testimonials, the boys each took a gopher snake (which looked slightly like a rattler) out of their bag, held it in the air and began a Hottentots dance toward the center aisle.

Quite a drama ensued. Half of the congregation was climbing on the benches and shouting, "Save us Jesus!" The other half was climbing over each other and the benches to get out of the tabernacle, shouting phrases which cannot be printed here. The neighboring town no doubt heard the screams. The commotion so startled the boys that they dropped their trophies and ran. Brother Foote, understanding his role to be that of saving his congregation, took his pistol with the carved cross on it and began to shoot at the snakes.

It is a good thing that it was the last night of the revival because all was over. No one even speculated as to the number of conversions made.

It was the last time the gun with the cross on the handle was ever fired. It could not even hit a harmless, swiveling snake.

It was the last time that Brother Foote was ever asked to hold a revival.

When their fathers finally caught up with them, it became the last that either of the boys was able to sit down for a long, long time without pain. They decided to join the Methodists.

The Traveling Toy Trunk

The little trunk had been relegated to an inconspicuous spot underneath a side table of the antiques booth. It obviously had once belonged to a little girl a long time ago. The piece was just large enough to house a doll and other treasures of a child. The painted flowers were faded, the stays were broken and some were missing. Why it had even been brought to the show was something of a mystery because the toy trunk would not possibly bring more than a few dollars. It's only worth was its history and where it once had been.

The item had originally belonged to an eight year old girl by the name of Cora Ella Harris. The toy trunk had been given to her in preparation for the move her family was making in 1878 from a farm in Georgia to a place called Weatherford, Texas. Still reeling from the throes of the War Between the States, Cora's father and his brother had decided to move their families out of the troubled South to a place where new beginnings could be made. The men had traveled ahead with their wagons filled with furniture, and herded what few cattle they had behind the wagons. It was to be a difficult journey taking several weeks. The wise decision had been made that the women and children would follow on the train after the men had located and made adequate preparations for their lives to march forward.

And so it was that after three months, the men sent for their families. Cora and her mother, Aunt Catherine and her baby, who was almost two, and Cousin Bonnie, who was six, all boarded the train with much ado and enthusiasm. None of them had ever been on a train before. Rarely had the two women even traveled out of the county. What an ensemble they were, two young women and three little girls, valises, food baskets, sacks of things to entertain the girls and the little doll trunk.

The women had spent quite some time preparing the little trunk for the journey. If everything else were lost or stolen, who would bother with a child's toy such as the trunk? That was their contention anyway. Carefully they removed the cloth lining and hidden what meager funds they had in the false bottom which they created for that purpose. Next they camouflaged the few pieces of silver they had in stuffed dolls. Needless to say, they kept a careful watch on this inconspicuous piece of luggage.

With much ado and tearful goodbyes, the journey began, and the first day and night went rather well. The girls became more and more familiar with the setting and "rowdiness" was a polite word for their behavior. The conductor, disgusted with the children's behavior, became belligerent, issuing occasional threats.

The train rolled along at a tedious pace and the girls became bored with counting the cows grazing in the passing pastures. Most of the seats in the passenger car were vacant and a game of hide-and-seek seemed harmless enough. The conductor did not really seem to mind too much because he had struck up an acquaintance with a traveling whiskey salesman. Both men were relishing in their new friendship, especially as they began to sample and test the products which the salesman had in his case.

The game of hide-and-seek evolved into relay races up and down the aisle, as the noise level rose considerably. The baby screamed because she was not allowed to join in the races. Periodic chides from the conductor and glares from the other travelers only challenged Bonnie and Cora to test the limits. As the evening wore on, the conductor and his new found friend were overcome by their need for naps. The girls had calmed somewhat, but when the very large hat of another sleeping passenger fell from the overhead rack into the aisle, the temptation was greater than two little girls could bear.

The giant hat was covered with black plumes and a festive red satin bow was its crowning glory. Cora picked it up and tried it on and pretended to Bonnie, "I am a famous actress on my way to the theater." She began to strut down the aisle with wiggling hips modeling the fancy chapeau.

"Take that off, Cora, before that lady wakes up." warned Bonnie. However, the word of caution fell on the deaf ears of Cora. In fact, she was having so much fun with the glamorous hat with its floating plumes that Bonnie finally grabbed it off Cora's head and began her own style show. During these playful antics the girls began to notice the sleeping conductor and his friend.

"I think he must be dead," implied Cora.

"Good!" exclaimed Bonnie.

"We need to be sure," said Cora, "before we tell mama."

"I really hate to have to do this, but there is only one way to be positive," decided Bonnie. With determined drama, she pulled the long hatpin from the hat and stuck the sleeping conductor's rear with the weapon.

As it turned out, the conductor was not dead at all. Actually he showed great signs of life as he yanked the hat off Bonnie's head with one hand and pulled the emergency cord with his other hand.

"Off!" he shouted and pointed to the door. The train came to a screeching halt. The two women and the three little girls were literally thrown off the train with all the baggage, including the little trunk.

The travesty occurred in the middle of the night

and their circumstances were made even drearier by a slight rain. The women believed themselves to be somewhere in the hills of Arkansas. Should they wait by the side of the tracks for another train? Or make a shelter? Finally leaving their entire luggage by the side of the track, except the little trunk, they began to walk along the track. At last they saw some sort of a dim light on the side of the hill, so they made their way toward it. The light proved to be from a lantern in a crudely built cabin.

Knocking hesitantly, they were apprehensive when a tall, thin black man opened the door. He was as startled to see them as they were to see him. He was a good man and a gentleman. Much to their surprise, he welcomed them into his dwelling and prepared some coffee and sandwiches. Pallets were made for the girls on the floor, as the adults pondered the possibilities.

Early the next morning the black man hitched up his mules to the wagon and loaded the party in it. They drove to get their trappings which had been left by the side of the track. Creakily the old wagon with its curious cargo made its way toward a water storage tank where the trains had to stop. There was a small depot there with a station attendant. At the edge of the clearing, the wagon was hidden in the trees and the black man went by himself to explain the situation to the attendant and seek direction.

The depot was half filled with miners and loggers who sought refuge from the cold night. Most were drunk.

"It would be quite dangerous to bring these women into the depot. Many of these men have not even seen a woman in months and in the men's drunken condition, there is no telling what might happen," puzzled the attendant. After some speculation, it was determined that the women and children could be locked in a storeroom on the back of the depot. The station attendant planned to somehow get them on the train that evening. So the stranger from the hillside quietly smuggled the scared party from Georgia into the storeroom. The door was locked so that no one could either come or go. The travelers, who only 24 hours before had been so filled with excitement and enthusiasm, huddled together in a dark storeroom, fearing for their safety.

Sometime during the middle of the day, the station attendant slipped them some food and something to drink. No feast was ever more palatable. Even the girls sensed the precariousness of their circumstances, and they were quieter than their mothers ever believed possible.

As the evening train screeched to a halt, the attendant hustled the entourage into the passenger car without much incident. What could have been in their hearts as the train headed toward Weatherford? Two total strangers had probably saved their lives. How ironic that they had gone by train because it was too difficult a journey for them to travel with their husbands in the wagons.

The families were safely and thrillingly united

in another day. As you might expect, a lawsuit was filed against the railroad. The settlement enabled the families to purchase good farms near Weatherford, Texas. Afterwards the little trunk reverted to its intended use. Hopefully everybody lived happily ever after, except the drunken conductor.

The White Lace Dress

It is to be doubted if any treasure at the antiques shows had required the skill of more advanced artisans than did the miniature portraits, especially those painted on ivory. Some of these renderings are truly masterpieces and under strong magnification even reflect the work of a one or two hair brush used for eyelashes and hair. Miniature portraits can also be found painted on china; others, in enamel on copper.

The custom dated back to the Seventeenth Century, but really became faddish in the Nineteenth Century. This was, of course, before the days of cameras and these treasures were given to men going off to war, a sweetheart who was traveling or by some gentleman who wished to be thought of often. Occasionally there would be found a memorial portrait with a lock of the deceased hair woven into a design in the back panel of the frame. Much intrigue was associated with some of these paintings. Men often carried watches or match safes with a hidden compartment in which they carried a portrait of their mistress. The most mysterious were the paintings of a single eye, so that if an illicit painting were found, no one could recognize for sure whose it was.

Portrait painting was a lucrative business and provided livelihood for numerous roving artists, no few of which were immigrants. During the cold months, the artists could work in the comfort of their own homes. Various settings were depicted, leaving only the faces unfinished. Then in the warmer months they could travel around the country and quickly fill in the faces. One such artist was a German immigrant by the name of A. Gustav who worked in the Philadelphia area. For a woman to be eternalized by this well-known artist was something of a status symbol, so he was always busy.

A. Gustav was commissioned to create such a portrait by a woman of some importance in Philadelphia. Her own posh apartment was to provide the setting. The woman's prized dress was of white lace and had cost untold sums, according to her. She even implied that it was done by the same designer who had made Mary Todd Lincoln's $5000 black lace gown. Of course, her portrait had to emphasize the dress.

The woman made the artist wait over an hour while she perfected her appearance. The maid offered the artist a cup of tea, but the woman's sharp voice came from the other room, "No tea. He is not here to socialize. He is here to work."

Much instruction was given to the veteran artist as how he was to proceed, what colors to use and which of her best features were to be emphasized. "I want this portrait to be a classic among those of the well-known and socially prominent," she chided.

She was haughty and arrogant, so A. Gustav thought, and he made sure that those qualities were reflected in the portrait. Unbelievably, she liked the portrait and evidently wished to be so perceived. He was not too surprised when a well-dressed gentleman showed up at the final sitting and paid his fee. They all shook hands and the artist departed happily. That was the end of the matter.

Some months later on a luscious spring day, A. Gustav knocked at the door of a prosperous farm house about thirty miles outside of Philadelphia. Explaining his purpose and showing examples of his artistry, he was hired to do a portrait of the lady of the manor. She thought it would make a wonderful gift for her husband whose livelihood caused him to travel a lot.

Whereas the woman was somewhat plain and not what anyone would call gorgeous, there was a quality of goodness and beauty about her that A. Gustav had seldom seen. It was a difficult sitting because three children kept running in and out demanding her attention. Obviously, she was much more concerned about their needs than she was about having her portrait painted.

A. Gustav saw her husband only once. However, it was an encounter that neither the husband nor A. Gustav would ever forget. The husband had come into the parlor to ask some question of his wife, but almost had an attack when he saw the artist. The color drained from his face, which took on the expression of a scared rabbit about to be shot.

Abruptly did he ignore the introduction of the artist. The husband brushed aside the extended hand of the artist. Almost running out of the parlor, he hoped he had departed before A.Gustav recognized him, but it was too late. The artist knew it was the same gentleman who had paid for the portrait of the haughty woman in the white dress in the posh Philadelphia apartment.

Discretion kept A. Gustav from showing any recognition or even hinting to the lady that he had met her husband previously. The circumstances belabored the artist considerably. This beautiful, charming woman, who adored both her children and her husband, was being betrayed by her husband and the haughty mistress. What could the artist do but keep his mouth shut?

The husband did not again make an appearance for the duration of the sitting. When it was at last finished, the artist made a rather strange request. "Do you mind," he asked the charming mother, "if I take this portrait with me? I would like to do it over with you in a more elaborate dress. If you do not like the changed picture, this one will still be yours."

"Well, how thoughtful," she replied. "Just so it is finished in time for Christmas." Gustav assured her that it would be and it was.

The new portrait on ivory depicted the lovely lady. All of the kindness and gentleness and love he had sensed in her were reflected in the portrait. Her wonderful qualities shone through brightly, illuminated by the gorgeous white lace dress he had painted on her. No wonder that the white lace dress was so perfect. It was the second time he had painted the gown, only this time with even more radiance.

She paid the artist. He signed the portrait and put the date, as was his usual custom. On the back of the portrait, he wrote the lady's name and underneath it put a strange inscription:

"Proverbs 31:10–31."

The gift was wrapped without the husband seeing the finished product. Christmas arrived with the usual amount of excitement and anticipation.

When the package was given to the errant husband and opened on Christmas morning, his face turned ashen. He turned as white as the dress in the portrait of his wife. Of course, he recognized the dress. He had paid handsomely for it. Was he about to pay for it again?

In a whispered voice he asked, "Where did you get that dress?"

Laughingly she explained, "That gorgeous gown is

a figment of the artist's imagination. He said it was identical to the famous dress of Mrs. Lincoln's. Do you like it?"

Had the artist told the woman about her husband's business trips to Philadelphia? Did she know about his mistress? "Well," her husband stammered, "I am sure that no dress has ever looked lovelier than that one does on you."

Not knowing exactly what to do, he took the portrait and left the room. In the quiet of his study, he noticed the scripture reference. For a long time he pondered the reading from Proverbs.

Summoning all the strength he could possibly muster, he took the original painting on ivory from a hidden compartment in his pocket watch. Holding a portrait in each hand, both of the same dress, but two different women, he walked to the fire place and carefully dropped the portrait of the mistress in the fire.

"What was that?" his smiling wife asked.

"Nothing," he responded, "Absolutely nothing." And he put his arms around his wife, as the Spirit of Christmas curled her arms around a father and mother and three happy children.

Toasting in Cranberry

Nothing could have been more beautiful and eye-catching than the set of six cranberry wine glasses. They had been washed to perfection and arranged on a mirrored plateau. Spotlights hit them just right, so that the gold in the cranberry glass reflected iridescently. The bowls had a gold rim around the top and it was decorated with tiny blue and pink enameled flowers. The bowls were proudly upheld by cut glass faceted stems. Close observation would show a signature which looked liked a tiny scratch but was the name of the maker, Moser. Originally there were twelve in the set and they had been costly a hundred years ago.

The set of twelve Moser stems had been a wedding

gift from the groom's family to Hayes and Molly. Little did his family ever dream of how offensive the gift would be to Molly's family. Her people were all active in the Church of Christ and were tee-totalers. Nothing could have seemed more inappropriate to them for such a sacred occasion as a wedding as anything that suggested alcohol.

Well, the day of the big event rolled around. The wedding was to take place in Molly's farm home at noon on the North side of town. Noon came and everyone was there from both families except Hayes and his brother, who was to be best man. One o'clock was sounded by the mantel clock, but still no Hayes. Lunch was burning, as well as Molly and two mothers. By two o'clock lunch was ruined and the conversations were strained.

A little after two, singing could be heard from down the road, as Hayes and his brother jauntily drove their buggy right up to the front gate, crushing some well-cultivated flowers as they did. To say that Hayes and his brother were "three sheets to the wind" is the most polite way of expressing their condition. Furthermore, they seemed totally unaware of the reason for their frosty, icy reception. What whispers went amongst those assembled are best left unremembered.

The two handsome young men were stumbling and staggering with song, and the songs were definitely not hymns. Their Prince Albert coats looked a little like they had dressed in them yesterday and so slept. Hair which might have been groomed when they left home now could have been mistaken for a homemade mop. The smiling Hayes looked at his brother and asked, "Why are they all looking so glum? This is a wedding. Let's celebrate!" Theirs were the sole countenances that were smiling or celebrating.

Hayes' mother, with a tone that would have chilled ice in winter, said to her son, "Let's go out on the back porch and let me help you freshen up a bit." Their conversation is not printable.

Molly's mother, mentally quoting all the scripture she could remember which might sustain her through this moment, finally settled on a quote from Shakespeare: "This, too, shall pass."

The bride assumed the stance and demeanor of a Greek statue. As if she were carved in gorgeous marble, there was neither emotion nor change in her gaze. Her thoughts were not to be read.

Most of the men were too angry, too amused, or too afraid of their wives to express anything but a straight face. The gathering was something like a bouquet of flowers that do not go well together, many varying blooms tightly bound in a cramped vessel. It was a wedding long to be remembered in the community.

The ceremony took place shortly thereafter, but there was no kiss from the bride. Hayes' family had brought champagne to toast the bride and groom and Molly's mother just winced as the bubbly was poured into the cranberry glasses. Nothing could have degraded the disastrous event further, or so she thought. With the dignity of a reigning queen, she announced, "Luncheon is served." And under her breath she muttered, "Two hours late and burnt."

What could be salvaged of lunch was finally presented and Molly filled a plate for Hayes, hoping that food might help. She placed his plate on the mantel because she realized he could not balance it on his knee in his celebratory state. However, much to her chagrin, someone brought him a glass of champagne and sat it by the plate.

The most exciting moment of the afternoon dawned when Hayes, trying to cut the burnt chicken, scooted it off his plate and across the parlor floor. In an effort to catch the chicken before it hit the floor, he somehow knocked the gorgeous wine glass from the mantle, so that from the very first day there were only eleven stems in the set.

Guests endeavored to clean up the mess with as little ado as possible, and to smooth matters over, Hayes' sister offered him another glass of champagne which he pleasantly accepted. At this juncture, Molly steadily walked across the room and in "steel magnolia" manners took the wine glass from Hayes and stated to his sister, "Hayes doesn't drink anymore."

Hayes rolled his eyes pleadingly at his brother, who was not in much better condition, but he heard Molly's ultimatum. He did not drink anymore! The eleven wine glasses were relegated to a shelf in the china cabinet and were not filled for many years. The stems were utilized when one of their sons miraculously graduated from college and were used again when their other son returned safely from WWII. For the most part, they just adorned the cabinet and collected compliments.

Hayes and Molly began to laugh about their wedding disaster about the time of their twenty-fifth anniversary. They made the decision to give each of their sons a pair of the cranberry glasses upon the event of each boy's wedding. This brought the set down to seven. The cranberry wine stems solicited many "ohs" and "ahs" because of their rarity and beauty.

The glasses were last used by Molly and Hayes on their Fiftieth Anniversary. The saga of their wedding was shared in the midst of hilarity. They toasted one another and fifty years together.

Their home was dismantled not too long after that event. We simply do not know the provenance of the glasses and how a set of six came to be a featured treasure at an antiques show in Houston in the 1980's. Nor do we know what happed to the seventh glass. That part of the story is simply missing. Perhaps it was sold as an orphan or maybe it was broken in transport. The remaining six themselves had quite a history to reveal.

The set solicited numerous comments throughout the show but none could equal that of an elegantly dressed woman who looked a little as if she had been sprayed with diamonds. She became distraught and began to cry, which shortly evolved into a wail. There had been a big flood in Houston only a few months before and the collections and loves of many enthusiasts had been devastated. A large percentage of the populace had suffered from the calamity, but this woman was lamenting as if she were the only one who had suffered a loss.

"Every time I see cranberry glass, I remember my

cabinet of the finest examples which were all lost. I will never collect anything again. It is just too painful and it is unfair that I spent forty years devoted to that collection only to have it wiped out in an afternoon." She carried on with this obnoxious tirade, "Insurance cannot mend my broken heart." Everybody was relieved when she left the booth. She repeated the performance in other booths during the afternoon. She made a complete donkey out of herself and her braying even sounded a little like one.

Less than an hour later a modestly dressed patron studied the cranberry wine set admiringly. She came back for the third time to consider the glasses. Happily she related to the dealer, "I received a nice check from the insurance company for my flood damage. This is the first time in my entire life that I have had money to spend on luxurious beauty. I am trying to decide if I want just one grand piece or try to replace several things that were lost throughout the house."

Finally reaching a decision she gleefully smiled, "These glasses are the most beautiful things I have ever seen. The purchase will take my entire insurance check, but these are what I want."

The startled dealer began to cautiously wrap the set and queried, "What will you do with them?"

"Oh," she poured forth with excitement, "I already have many plans. My husband and I will toast with them every afternoon. I can hardly wait to invite my neighbors over for a glass of wine. Just seeing the sun shine through them on my glass shelf in the dining room will bring joy every time I pass by them."

Same set of glasses, same flood, same insurance checks but what a contrast in reactions to an unfortunate happening. The dealer could not help but smile as he thought, "At long last these cranberry wine glasses are in the home for which they were created." Who knows what their future might unfold?

The Purloined Possum

Examples of "Tramp Art" can often be found at the antiques shows. Usually, they are rather simple handmade articles constructed of supplies which were readily available. Scraps of wood provided foundations for artistic renderings of the wood burning needle and pocketknife creations. Really fancy manifestations might boast sea shells or porcupine quills. This type of folk art represents a significant era of American history, the Great Depression, during which citizens were hard-pressed to acquire a few dollars.

Before the term "homeless people" became politically correct, wanderers were called hobos or bums or tramps. Many lived in makeshift camps under bridges or near railroads. Often they could be seen bumming rides on boxcars or with thumbs up near rural highways. Some went from house to house endeavoring to sell the crudely made objects, even being willing to trade them for a meal or shelter. The back porch steps were popular eating places.

Many jokes, stories and fables developed about the hobos. A few may have been apocryphal, but most were fables in an age when storytelling was the evening entertainment before radio or TV commanded our attention. My grandfather, who everybody called Pappy, was a master story teller and entertained the grandchildren on a summer's night after the milking and supper had been completed.

On a super night, we might even have a freezer of homemade ice cream. Always an old quilt could be spread on the grass, fireflies could be caught in a fruit jar and chiggers could have a feast. A myriad of sagas existed about the stars or our family history but my favorite story, and I think Pappy's, was about two hobos. I have no idea if he concocted the tale, if he read it somewhere, if it is true or what we might just call "oral tradition." The antics and expressions and noises which we grandchildren mimicked added to the fun.

Two hungry, weary hobos had tramped the woods until they could go no farther. As they dropped into a restful location by an old hollow log, they were surprised to see some big eyes staring at them from within, and the eyes proved to belong to a fat possum. One hobo getting at each end of the log, they were able to capture their dinner. With much ado, they prepared their feast and constructed a rack on which to cook their prize.

Now it takes a long time to cook a fat, greasy possum, and while one hobo was roasting it over their fire, the other one lay down and went to sleep. In fact, you could hear his stomach growling because they really had nothing to eat for two days. The other hobo rotated the possum, cooking it to perfection. When it was deliciously ready, he decided to take just one little taste before his partner awakened. That little taste led to another little taste and then another and then another until the chef realized with a grimace that he had eaten the entire possum while his cohort slept

What to do? Could he catch another possum? Could he concoct a tale about it falling into the fire? Or maybe one about wild dogs grabbing it from the spit and running?

Carefully he staged the perfect solution. He placed the possum bones in front of the sleeping man. He took the grease and fat from the possum and rubbed it ever so gently on the sleeper's hand and even on his lips and all around his mouth. Then he tiptoed over to the other side of the fire and pretended to be asleep.

At last the sleeping hobo awoke and tasted the possum on his lips. He looked down at his hands; all covered with possum grease, and wiped them on his pants, as he thoughtfully studied the bones in front of him.

Seizing the moment the pretend sleeper drowsily queried his puzzled friend, "Well, how did you like the possum?" And the duped hobo responded by licking his lips, rubbing his stomach and saying, "You know, I think that the best possum I ever 'et."

At this point we grandchildren licked our lips and rubbed our stomachs and affirmed, "That's the best possum we ever 'et."

The Petit Point Pillow

Much interest was shown in the petit point pillow in a corner of the antiques booth. Its uniqueness was that the design was a street scene rather than the usual floral or geometric patterns. The colors were in soft blues and greens and depicted a house on a lovely street. If you carefully studied the scene, you might notice the street sign, in tiny little letters, bore the name VERONICA and on the house could be discerned the numbers 1936. The house was a simile of the maker's home. Veronica was the name of the German-Jewish teenager who had labored all one summer on this magnificent work of art for her "hope chest." The house numbers 1936 indicated the year the piece was made. Little did she anticipate the importance of the role that pillow was to play in her life.

Even though the Jewish people had been settled in Germany for a few hundred years, the mistreatment and persecution of them had begun long before Hitler. In a myriad of manners, they had been declared outcasts. Under the Third Reich, all Jewish businesses had been boycotted. All Jewish identification papers were stamped with a large yellow J, and one law even required that all Jews must add either "Isaiah" or "Sarah" to their name. Then the time came when the Jews were being deported and sent to the gas chambers.

Veronica's family was rather prominent in a small town in central Germany. Her father had owned a small bank and some wealth had been accumulated. However, the father was a smart man and could see the handwriting on the wall. He realized that it was only a matter of time until their family would be dissipated. What to do? There were three daughters. Veronica, age 17, and two younger sisters ages 10 and 8. All of them looked very Jewish, except Veronica, who was a blue-eyed blonde and had never had any difficulty passing as an Aryan German.

Those parents discovered the real meaning of "soul searching." Most of the children were being sent to camps in Hungary, so the parents believed the lives of their two younger daughters would be spared. Some of the adults were sent to slave regimens and others to places unknown, which was polite euphemism for gas chambers. The parents were uncertain about their own future, but planned and prayed, if possible, to insure the future of their daughters.

A dramatic and traumatic scheme surfaced. The thought was that if Veronica could escape with access to the modest fortune, then when the strife was ended she could locate her younger sisters and take care of them. The banker liquidated all the assets at his disposal. Much was invested in small diamonds and the rest secreted to a Swiss bank account. The diamonds were purloined into the cord around the petit point pillow. Veronica's mother took apart the teenager's bra strap and embroidered the number of the Swiss bank account on the inside of the strap, working the number into the decoration on the bra.

The only piece of investment art the family owned that Veronica could carry was a small Oriental antique carpet worth a few thousand dollars. With some old quilts, the carpet was made into a sort of primitive sleeping bag, which she was able to carry as a backpack.

No words could possibly express the pain and agony of that Jewish family as they sent their daughter into the oblivion of the forest near their home. It was a heavy emotional burden for a teenager to bear. The farewell was frightening, more frightening and bewildering than a funeral. The father hugged his daughter with that special love which can exist only between fathers and daughters. "I am so proud of you and love you so much," he whispered as he choked back the tears.

The mother's embrace lasted much longer. Trying her best to give some word of significance to her departing daughter, she could only utter, "You may have to assume the role of mother for your sisters. Teach them what you know I would want them to learn and help them to discover the best that is within them."

The younger sisters had not been told about the scheme. They only knew Veronica was off on a camping trip, and that something very serious was taking place. Wanting to be a part of the loving farewell, one of the younger sisters secretly slipped her treasured Star of David necklace into Veronica's coat pocket.

The heart-broken teenager looked back only once, but the pain was too great to give more than a glance. As a matter of fact, it was the last time Veronica ever saw either of her parents.

Veronica slowly made her way toward the French border. Of course, she carried no papers because hers would have indicated that she was Jewish. Sleeping in the homemade sleeping bag with her head resting on the petit point pillow, she somehow survived all right in the woods for about two days. Then she became ill, as one might well expect.

Seeing a farm house and a barn filled with hay, she slept there on the third night. The farmer spotted her the next morning and called his wife to bring some food.

"Why are you sleeping in our barn?" the farmer's wife asked.

Veronica was improvising some sort of story when the woman bent to pick something shiny off the floor of the barn. It was the Star of David necklace which the little sister had lovingly placed in her pocket.

"My whole story is right there in your hand," Veronica said in a soft, hopeful voice. The farmer and his wife understood.

The kind woman took care of Veronica for a few days until she was nursed back to health. The couple was not Jewish, but they were sympathetic with the plight of the Jews. The family was aware they were putting their own safety at peril by allowing the girl to stay in their barn. Nevertheless, they risked arrest because they were good people, as were many Germans.

"Please throw that necklace in the well," advised the farmer, "before it cost you your life." And so it was done.

Upon her recuperation, Veronica's pilgrimage began again. A close encounter came when some Gestapo had stopped her and asked for identification papers. Of course, she had none. Her heart was pounding, as she fumbled in her backpack pretending to look for the non-existent papers.

A woman across the street witnessed the happenings and suddenly screamed at the top of her lungs. "Catch that kid. He stole my purse." She pointed to the corner away from Veronica. "Be careful" she warned the officers. "That dog with him may be rabid. He bites."

As the officers were distracted, Veronica disappeared. The scene evolved as the woman had most likely intended. She even showed the officers some blood on her leg where she said the dog had bitten her. By the time they were finished consoling the screaming woman, Veronica was long since gone.

Several perils could be told, but Veronica was finally helped into France by a young SS official who felt sorry for her, never suspecting her Jewish background. Fears were somewhat alleviated after she crossed the French border, but physical circumstances were arduous. There was trouble in getting anyone to purchase one of the diamonds from her because she was unidentified. Proper merchants were leery about such a purchase, and the average person during those war torn years had little use for a diamond, even if they had the knowledge to negotiate such a transaction. Her father had not anticipated the difficulty to be encountered by a young traveler with no identification papers. One night she even bartered a quarter carat diamond for a meal and a hotel room.

It took her about six weeks to make her way across France and find herself in London, which was her ultimate destination. There she believed that money could be claimed from the Swiss account, but again, the lack of proper identification kept the banks from honoring her requests. The diamond supply in her petit point pillow had been depleted and in desperation she liberated the antique carpet from the homemade sleeping bag, which had been her bed for many weeks.

Cleaning the rug as best she could, it was offered to

a dealer in antique carpets. Brazenly did he offer her $15 dollars for the investment piece. Without even responding, she rolled up her rug and left his office. An auction house agreed to offer the rare carpet, and she realized almost $20,000 from its sale.

With her money she began to deal in antique silver. There was much available during WWII in London and she did have some limited expertise in the silver trade. Becoming a regular vendor in the silver vaults, which London had built to preserve its treasures, Veronica did well and began to establish herself in business.

The matter of the Swiss bank account was still a problem. In fact, almost five years elapsed until she found a lawyer who would help her. He was a relatively young man who had the patience and expertise to help her authenticate her right to the money. Day after day they tried to access the account. Results were ultimately victorious.

By the end of WWII, Veronica and the young lawyer were wed. How she found her sisters in Hungary is another story. Sufficient to say, the pillow perched in a prominent spot on the living room sofa of a posh London flat for many years just to remind the residents of whom they really were and the price that was paid for peace and happiness.

Mislaid Treasures

It had to be one of the ugliest pieces of furniture God ever allowed to be created. In fact, the hall tree was so distasteful that it had sat in a barn for over thirty years and was used to hang harnesses and hold tools. The sort of image that is conjured in many minds when the word "antique" is uttered was exemplified by this horror. The barn was a good place for it because few modern families would have wanted it in their home. It was in that barn that an antiques dealer had found the hall tree and cleaned it up.

One young couple was particularly intrigued with it because the man commented that it was exactly like one his grandmother had. Many antiques are sold on the basis of sentimentality, so the dealer gave the enthusiastic pair special attention. The man finally asked the dealer if the hall tree had a secret hiding place, as did his grandmother's.

"She always hid candy or coins or some special treat for us in the drawer and when we visited her, that secret hiding place was our first stop," he remembered.

"Well," responded the dealer, "To the best of my knowledge this piece does not have such a secret hiding place. Where was the drawer?"

The young man pointed to three little knobs on either side of the mirror. "If you loosened the top and bottom knobs, the middle knob would pull out the drawer," the young man explained.

With glee and enthusiasm, and with the antiques dealer hoping his hall tree was not being ruined, the knobs were loosened and a drawer was discovered. To the absolute astonishment of all watching, and several had gathered by now for the demonstration, there was a prize inside the cavity. In fact, a rather valuable piece of jewelry in a fitted velvet case all covered with dust and grime was revealed. Inside the case were an emerald necklace and some diamond earrings. Of course, the spectators were all elated.

Robert M. Turner

Had they known the pain and suffering which had been caused by that jewelry, they might have been apprehensive. The jewelry, which was worth a few thousand dollars, had caused untold misery. The hall tree had originally belonged to an old maid aunt who dwelt in her large, rambling family home. Having no children of her own, she had promised the family heirloom jewelry to her two nieces but had neglected to tell them where she kept the pieces.

The two girls both thought the other had purloined the jewelry. A huge family onslaught ensued. After some months of accusation and mud slinging, they developed an idea that the jewelry had been stolen by a male cousin, who was angry because he had not been remembered in the aunt's will. The ill feelings and rift were so serious among the family members that they never had anything to do with each other after that. For over thirty years they had not spoken to each other and had made hatred at home in their hearts.

An insurance company finally paid the claim for stolen jewelry, after a small lawsuit. The money was divided amongst the relatives, but nothing ever healed the wounds and they were all robbed of warm relationships unnecessarily.

Earthly treasures are sometimes over valued. A family had been cheated out of more than one treasure which was rightfully theirs for over thirty years. Which lost treasure had cost them more?

"If I purchase the hall tree," the young customer winked, "does the jewelry go with it?"

The dealer looked absolutely shocked, "Why," he attested, "I would not dream of parting with this magnificent piece of Victorian craftsmanship. In fact, I think you could say that it is my favorite item in the booth."

Flour Sacks and Feed Bags

Most of the younger patrons who wandered past the stitchery booth at the antiques show did not even pause to give it a serious glance. After all, how could any one who had been equipped with a credit card possibly identify with rickrack, penny candy, nickel soda and the myriad of miracles from the magical caverns of the dime store?

Most of the handmade articles in the stitchery booth did have a certain homemade quality about them. There were those odd sunbonnets with their cardboard stays. Only after wealthy world travelers began to return with tanned skin from exotic locations did it become fashionable to be in the sun.

The bonnets had been designed so that farm women could work in the garden and outside without telltale freckles or browned skin. One sunbonnet was even made of black silk and had most likely been used by someone in mourning.

Quilts and braid rugs all boasted scraps from farm wardrobes. Many items in the booth were made from a coarse cotton material and had originally been sacks for flour and sugar. A ten pound flour sack was just the right size to make a tea towel. Two of them could produce a pillowcase. After all, young girls did have a hope chest for which to prepare. These flour sacks provided good practice exercises. It was widely rumored that some families bleached the sacks and made underwear out of them. However, no one ever admitted to being that poor or uncouth.

When the USA entered into WWII, the government confiscated all hemp to manufacture ropes and camouflage netting for the troops. This posed quite a problem for those who sold cow and chicken feed and seed to the farmers because those products had always marketed in burlap bags. One of the most brilliant schemes developed which not only sacked those products but answered other needs as well.

Giant sacks were made from the cotton material which had previously been used for flour. To help sales and to provide fabric which was scarce during wartimes, these large feed bags were printed in attractive floral designs and colorful motifs. A one hundred pound feed bag could make a small tablecloth and three of them rendered a pair of pajamas for a child. Occasionally little girls showed up at school in dresses from the same fabric. Many a farmer was pressured into buying some product which he could have done without because his wife needed one more feed sack in the poppy design to complete her kitchen curtains. These marvelous sacks are unique phenomena in our marketing history.

The long colorful aprons which had been made from feed sacks were of a special design developed by farm women. The garments tied around the waist and hung almost to the ground. Long cavernous pockets were included for holding shears or a penknife. As she went about her day, the apron could be pulled up to form a sort of cloth basket. In this she could carry the eggs she had gathered or fresh roasting ears or tomatoes. On a special day, the apron basket might even carry roses. Many a baby chick, which otherwise might have frozen in cold weather, had been transported to the electric light incubator in those aprons.

During WWII our nation was united in the war effort. People raised victory gardens and took acid and burned German hallmarks from fine china. Cheap Japanese items were often trashed because people did not even want such evil goods in their homes. Auction sales were held to buy war bonds. A box of hard to find shotgun shells might well necessitate the winner purchasing a $100 war bond. A five pound bag of sugar or some meat tokens or gasoline stamps were always quick sellers. Almost everyone did something to help our soldiers.

One small town in North Texas decided to have a banquet and auction certain rarities for the war effort. The entire town was encouraged to attend the banquet which was to be held at the Methodist Church. The meal was to be prepared by the ladies of the Missionary Society. Now in that august group were two girls, both named Myrtle, who had grown up together on neighboring farms. Before school buses, they had ridden the same dray wagon to school everyday for years carrying their lunches in syrup buckets which had been decorated.

One Myrtle had married a school teacher. Their lifestyle was meager, usually barely making ends meet. The other Myrtle had married the town's most prominent lawyer and had become without question the town's leading social attraction. Behind their backs, the other ladies of the Missionary Society called them "Poor Myrtle" and "Rich Myrtle" in order to distinguish between them when they gossiped about the two. There were usually a few eyebrows to be raised because there was much competition in the long history between the two Myrtles.

Now, Poor Myrtle was in charge of the kitchen for the dinner and Rich Myrtle was to be in charge of decorations and table settings. Poor Myrtle had stood at the church kitchen stove since seven o'clock on the morning of the big fundraiser. Rich Myrtle sauntered in about four o'clock in her new Neiman Marcus frock and began to make all sorts of suggestions. Her advice ranged from the seasoning in the potatoes to facing the knife blade toward the plate. As Rich Myrtle said, "We cannot have people coming from churches all over town and think that we are improper or don't know how things are supposed to be done."

This unsolicited bantering and advice-giving pervaded the kitchen ambiance for the afternoon, as well as providing a little entertainment for the other ladies of the Missionary Society. Matters reached a crux when Rich Myrtle walked into the kitchen and requested all of the women to take a moment before the banquet to comb their hair and freshen up a bit.

Now Poor Myrtle was standing at the deep sink up to her elbows in dishwater and suds. Rich Myrtle was standing at the kitchen door not wanting to get anything splashed on her new dress. Poor Myrtle could take no more and she raised a pan full of soap suds and shouted, "Oh, shut up, Myrtle. I knowed you when you wore flour sack drawers."

The expression "dead silence" took on new meaning. Rich Myrtle stood framed in the doorway with her hands on her hips and a look on her face that would have defeated Hitler himself. Poor Myrtle, still holding the soapy pan defiantly glared, not giving an iota. The rest of the Missionary Society moved slowly backward clinging to the cabinets. The pregnant pause, which lasted only a few seconds but seemed like minutes, could have produced almost anything.

The two lifelong acquaintances had finally reached an impasse.

That particular phase of the war was ended when Rich Myrtle broke into a smile and addressed Poor Myrtle, "I had forgotten flour sack drawers. Do you really remember them?"

Poor Myrtle conceded, "Remember them? I am still wearing them." Tension took a vacation and laughter reigned.

Rich Myrtle went over to Poor Myrtle and removed the dishwasher's apron and donned it herself over her Neiman-Marcus dress. "You go rest and have a cup of coffee. I still know how to wash dishes." The Missionary Society was never quite the same after that!

They are all gone now, the people and the treasures, the Myrtles and the Missionary Society. Dime stores, war bond auctions, feed bag aprons and flour sack drawers will all be forgotten, but so far nothing has arisen in our spectacular society that can take their places!

After Midnight

Steve became an antiques dealer by accident; at least it certainly was not his plan. He was without income when his grandmother died and left him her modest residence in an old neighborhood. The house was crammed with a lifetime of collecting. Her tastes had been exquisite even if her budget were not.

To make a long story short, he began to sell her furnishings out of necessity. Quickly did he pick up the jargon and trends of the antiques trade, and he was really quite good at it. In fact, within a year he had become a rather respected dealer at the shows. The women all liked to talk to him because he was young and good looking. His baby blue eyes and slightly uncombed hair had helped him to make more than a few sales.

As he was loading his van to go to the Atlanta show, the neighbor's cat, which was the bane of Steve's existence, kept climbing into the van. The cat's name was "Midnight" and it fit because the creature was coal black. The neighbor loved the cat, and the cat loved Steve. Steve hated cats, especially Midnight. Cats, however, have a special calling to people who do not care for them. Midnight understood Steve to be a challenge to be cultivated.

Every time Steve threw Midnight out of the truck, Midnight bounded back and rubbed against Steve's leg and purred pathetically. Finally, in desperation, Steve threw the cat back in the neighbor's yard and prayed that his neighbor did not see him abusing his pet. Steve finished loading the van in peace and had a rather uneventful drive to Atlanta.

As usual, he hired loading help to transport his merchandise to his booth. You can sense his utter amazement when one of the loading boys asked, "What do you want us to do with the cat?" There in the front seat of the van perched the black cat. Decorum prevents us from printing Steve's language here.

What to do? Should he telephone the neighbor and tell him where his cat was? If he did he knew it would be the end of a neighborhood friendship. Should he simply turn the cat loose in Atlanta? How could the neighbor ever know? On the other hand, how would he ever be able to look the neighbor in the face? The solution came when Steve found a long piece of yellow velvet ribbon which he tied around the cat's neck and the other end to the leg of a table. He decided that he would say nothing, get home after dark, and simply turn the cat loose. Midnight would then reinstate himself into his habitant.

The plan might have worked if another dealer had not brought his terrier to the show during setup. The dog eyed the cat and nature began to take its course. The yellow ribbon was easily pulled from the table leg and a chase began all over the floor of the show during set up time. Table covers were pulled by the two animals and antiques could be heard clinking as they were jostled by the chase. Never have you heard such screams as dealers endeavored to protect their merchandise from the critters. The animals chased under tables and once Midnight hopped on top of a table as the terrier barked ferociously. It had to be the most exciting setup in the history of antiques shows.

Even though the drama lasted only a few minutes, it seemed like hours to Steve. He was mortified! On top of the embarrassment, he knew he could be held liable for any items broken during the fray. He took the cat to the van and locked the vehicle. That night he again pondered the situation.

His conscience would not allow him to leave the cat in the van for three days, so he purchased a collar and leash. Slipping the leash under the leg of a chair defined the cat's roaming activity. It did cause Steve to wince when he viewed the cat arranging himself on the Seventeenth Century French chair, which was Steve's most expensive piece. The only thing he could get the cat to eat was fried chicken from the concession stand. So for the duration of the show Steve cat-sat, leaving the booth occasionally to walk the cat outside and feeding him fried chicken with more regularity than Steve ate himself. Never had the cat had so much attention. Numerous customers stopped to play with him. Midnight basked in the attention.

The show was finally over and Steve returned to his neighborhood with the cat in the front seat, behaving as if he were co-pilot. As Steve pulled into his driveway he almost wrecked the van because of what he saw sitting on top of his neighbor's flower urn on the front porch. There was Midnight just exactly where he usually was, preparing to welcome Steve home.

Steve eyed the cat in his passenger seat and slowly realized he had just given a stray cat a fabulous weekend in Atlanta. Undivided attention from the customers, unlimited fried chicken and a cushion of a $2000 chair had all contributed to the most glorious few days of the animal's existence. Steve's mumbling and what he called the cat would have caused his grandmother to turn over in her grave.

Something must have been established between Steve and the cat, because the cat became his traveling companion and a permanent decoration of his booth. People did sometimes think it peculiar that the cat's name was "Hypocrite."

The Miracle of a Rose

Filled with figural napkin rings, the glass case on the front table of the booth always attracted worshippers. Furthermore, there was a definite class distinction among the napkin rings. The largest and usually the most expensive of the cluster sat on the top shelf of the case. Those that were cute and pretty but still affordable adorned the second shelf. The losers and those with worn silver and common heritage were relegated to the bottom shelf and saw little action. Also displayed there were those that dealers politely called "marriages." They were of illegitimate conception and made by soldering together bits and pieces of broken rings. The little silver plated oddities are fun to collect and have helped many an awkward dinner party through the evening. The fad was an American fetish and became popular around 1870, lasting until well after the turn of the century.

Basically utilitarian, long before the days of paper napkins, when people might use the same cloth napkin for several meals, the funny little holders distinguished your napkin from Grandpa's with the tobacco juice, or Johnnie's with jelly stains or Mary Lou's who was always blowing her nose in her napkin. They were not sterling because a family who could afford sterling would have probably had fresh napkins for each meal. In fact, they were considered rather gauche, but fun nonetheless.

After the antiques show closed one evening and the case had been covered with a dust cloth, two of the top shelf rings, the giraffe under the palm tree and the monkey in the three-cornered hat playing a drum, were discussing how nice it was to be top shelf.

"Popularity is such a burden," sighed the giraffe.

"Well, when rings are handled as much as we are, it is always an added responsibility to keep shiny and be free of fingerprints," bemoaned the monkey with the funny hat. They believed that because they were from abroad and represented foreign cultures they were far superior to the domestic ilk.

The Rip Van Winkle ring looked condescendingly down at them because he was the tallest and bore the most expensive price tag. "To be the most collectible napkin ring is a real honor, and you two should maintain your dignity and relish in the honor of being top shelf," chided Rip Van Winkle.

The ring with the crossed Civil War rifles on the second shelf could not help but overhear the boastings. "Well," he shouted upward, "I once belonged to Col. Pickens himself." Of course, he did not mention that no one was ever quite sure of what he was a colonel, but the euphemism was respected. Was he really as old as the Civil War?

The ring with the books and an owl with glass eyes claimed he had once been used by a famous lawyer named Clarence Barrow, and the rest of the rings just shrugged with disgust at his bravado. The ring with the violin and the sheet music related her experiences with an orchestra conductor and the ring with the cockatoo had been utilized for years by a woman named Lady Bird. Oh, the sagas they revealed!

The beautiful lady who upheld a vase demurely voiced, "I would like to tell you my most romantic servitude (she was top shelf so they listened with some respect). A group of us customarily sat on the white starched tablecloth of a boarding house. I served the needs of the new fifth grade school teacher. Beaus were scarce in that little town and we were elated when a young banker appeared at the table. His napkin holder was a very friendly ring of a baseball player with bat and ball. We all did whatever we could to get them together, but nothing worked. One evening the teacher placed a luscious rose in my vase which she had plucked from a neighbor's garden."

The young man admired it and said, "I would

certainly like to see that garden. Where does this fabulous garden grow?"

"After supper, I will be glad to show it to you if there is still light," the fifth grade teacher cooed. They left hand-in-hand and when they returned giggling it was much too dark to see the roses, but they must have stopped to smell them because that was the beginning of romance. In fact, the baseball player and I were taken to their new home after they were married. We were happy there for many years." All the rings responded with "ahs" and there were even a couple of tears splattered on shelf two.

"I, too, am familiar with boarding houses and spent almost all my existence there," chimed in the ring with the cupid on the heart shaped platform. A majority of the other rings in the case thought she was really gaudy. The cupid on her ring even held two more hearts. "I belonged to Miss Clara who was a real romantic and often indulged herself in sentimentality. She often touched me kindly with dreamy fingers. Miss Clara was a lonely soul and not too blessed in the looks department, but she kept trying."

On Valentine's Day, Miss Clara executed her plan. Having taken her India ink pen, she put her initials on one silver heart and Mr. Rathjen's initials on the other and placed the ring with his napkin in it at his plate. He did not comment on it but smiled at her ever so slightly.

The next evening her ring was back at its place with the initials rubbed off. She did not know what that meant, but as the dishes were cleared, she saw the note under her plate in his handwriting. The little poem began so wonderfully and her heart began to race and then it broke. The poem proclaimed:

Roses are red,
Violets are blue.
I enjoy being single.
You might as well too!

Quickly did she cover the epistle. Supper was devoured in silence and the subject was never brought up again. "How sad," moaned two romantic rings, but only on the bottom shelf could a tear stain be found.

The Rip Van Winkle ring, top shelf, who considered himself president, boomed, "That is enough of this mindless gossip and chatter. We all need to get some rest so we can put our best qualities forward as we interview for new homes." He had always had a penchant for sleep anyway. So all three shelves yielded to his leadership and hopefully prepared for a better tomorrow.

Squirrel Stew in the Wash Pot

Well, the old wash pot had never looked that good before. Proudly did the pot sit filled with blooming geraniums in front of the antiques booth. The vessel had endured not only a good cleaning, but someone had blackened its surfaces to perfection. Setting up on three peg legs and with handles molded into its sides, the 15 gallon iron pot stood about 20" tall. This piece which would now decorate some patio had been of significance in the past and could it tell a few tales!

Almost every farm in Texas in the 1920's had such a utilitarian piece of equipment. Usually it was located somewhere between the back kitchen door and the well, and sat on a little circle of rocks on the sturdy legs. Eleven buckets of water from the well were required to fill it. Small fires would be ignited underneath and some homemade lye soap dissolved in the water. When the water was hot enough, clothes could be immersed for laundry.

The white clothes were always in the first pot and were jostled by the paddle from the churn to obtain a little circulation. After a few minutes, they would be lifted by some sort of stick into a #2 washtub filled with cold water and bluing. When they had cooled they could be wrung out and put into another tub of cold water to rinse. Next they were hung on the fence to dry. If a family were fancy enough, they might even have a clothesline. Mondays were traditionally wash days and all available family members were enlisted. In the air was the smell of pinto beans and ham hock simmering because that was the Monday menu.

This particular wash pot with its festive hat of geraniums had belonged to a family with eight children. It had cleaned over a forty year period from diapers to overalls, and its job had been done well. Of course, there was the time when Willie's mother told him to put more water in the wash pot, but he was distracted by the dog. So the pot boiled dry and all the clothes were burned or scorched. Willie's mother was a little burned herself and one might politely say that Willie's behind got a little scorched. It might be noted, he never let the wash pot boil dry again!

It served the family in modes other than just washing. Six or seven hens could be cooked in the boiling caldron at the same time. Thus the heat was kept out of the house and all the food was ready for canning at one time.

In the fall of the year a day or so after the hogs were slaughtered and hams hung in the smokehouse for the winter and the sausage was ground, the wash pot performed another vital function. It rendered all of the hog fat so that it could be made into soap. Some lye and sometimes borax were added. When the mixture reached satisfaction, it would be poured on the concrete floor of the smokehouse to harden. After drying a few days, pieces of soap could be broken from the slab and put in burlap sacks for use all year.

The pot had even been used once for apple bobbing at a Halloween party. However, of all its functions over its seventy years, none were more festive than the annual squirrel stew foray. The function had started at the little country church during the Depression when none of the farm families had enough means to go anywhere else but church for entertainment. The wash pot had been taken to the church in the old Model T Ford. The men went out and hunted for squirrels and the women and children had a good time all afternoon. What a marvelous event it was for everyone.

The Squirrel Stew Supper grew for year after year on the last Saturday in October. The crops were usually harvested by then and the people were ready for a good time. The festival, if it could be called that, evolved into the major fund raising event for the little country church. By the 1940's, six wash pots full of bubbling stew could be smelled in the church yard. The men would all go hunting after the morning milking was finished and the women would have spent the preceding days making cakes and breads and all sorts of goodies from their very best recipes.

People came from miles around for the annual squirrel stew happening. Little communities like Blue Ridge, Belles, Snow Hill, Boggy and Farmersville (aren't those wonderful names?) were often represented. They could either bring their own containers in which to take the stew home or they could eat it and the desserts in the picnic like epic.

Interestingly enough, they never made a charge for any of the food. Gallon glass jars were there for people to contribute whatever they could and the little church would realize between $2000 and $3000 each year. Now that does not seem like much to us, but keep in mind their preacher got paid $50 a month and was usually an SMU student. It is a miracle that the church survived financially or otherwise. The annual fund raiser was enough to keep the little country church going all year. But the real value was the good times and fellowship the squirrel stew suppers engendered.

It might look just like an old wash pot to people wandering through the antiques show, but it had kept a family clean for fifty years and a church going for thirty. Which of us has a more commendable provenance?

RECIPE FOR SQUIRREL STEW

Fresh well water

Cook 4 squirrels in wash pot until done.

Add 2 pounds chopped potatoes

Add 2 pounds chopped onions

Later add 2 cans (#2) cream corn

2 cans (#2) whole tomatoes

2 T. chili powder – 1 T. black pepper – 2T. salt

1 box macaroni

Cook for two hours over open fire.
Makes about three gallons.

Love at the Antiques Show

――――――

Doug was one of those regular customers at all three of the antiques shows which convened in Austin three times a year. For several years this young man had collected small glass inkwells and had accrued a notable array of the oddities. Always was he well-dressed and well-mannered and pleasant. Most of the dealers recognized him and were glad to have him in their booth. None of the dealers really knew who he was or got to know anything about him personally. Doug had, however, become friendly with an older couple, Earl and Gwen, who stocked their booth with colored glass antiques. Usually they had some inkwell for Doug to consider.

A flea market also was held in conjunction with the antiques show early Saturday morning before the antiques show opened at noon. Earl and Gwen tried to ferret out treasures there and always had fun sampling the homemade goodies. You can imagine their surprise when they spotted Doug set up as a dealer at the flea market! He had never been there before! Neatly arrayed was his collection of inkwells which he had been years in assembling.

He obviously did not wish to discuss why he was there, so Earl and Gwen did not pursue the subject. They purchased a large portion of his collection, some of which they had sold to him, for the price he asked without negotiation. Doug made the strange request that the check be made out to his son, and so it was done. Doug did not attend the antiques show that afternoon.

A few months later at the next antiques show, Doug did attend and asked Earl and Gwen if they would be interested in purchasing some other things he had in his car. Earl went out to the car, which happened to be a Mercedes, and bought all of the items Doug had there. Fortunately Doug understood that the dealers had to be able to make a profit, so Earl paid the asking price. Once again, Doug asked that the check be made out to his son. No invading questions were asked.

Doug did not attend the succeeding antiques show a few months later. Gwen and Earl wondered what had happened to him. At the next show which was not until the fall, Earl and Gwen were startled and saddened to see Doug in an emaciated condition. He was walking with a cane. Doug and a young boy carried a large leather case. Doug introduced the boy as his son.

Doug opened the case to reveal the most gorgeous tea service imaginable. The pieces were each a true work of art and rested proudly in their fitted satin case. The set was near museum quality and worth many thousands of dollars

With loving tones, Doug told Gwen and Earl, "This was a wedding gift to my grandparents from all their friends. It was handmade in Boston. I would like to sell it to you."

Earl hesitated. It was not the sort of merchandise they handled and certainly more costly than they usually bought. But there was another reason for his hesitancy to make the purchase.

"Doug," Earl cautiously pondered, "Shouldn't this set be saved for your son to inherit? It is so rare and such a treasure." Doug took some money from his pocket and asked his son to go to the concession stand and bring them all some cookies and coffee. Earl began to protest, but realized it was a ruse to send the boy out of earshot.

Doug took a deep breath and paused for some time. Asking Earl and Gwen for their absolute confidence, he shared with them that he had AIDS and most likely had only a rather short life expectancy.

"I am setting up a trust fund for my son's college education. He is going to need an education more than he will ever need a coffee service. Who knows what would ever happen to the set? The child might never get it anyway. My health expenses will somehow be taken care of but his college education may not be a reality unless I take care of it. A fair price for this wonderful set will push the amount in the trust into adequacy. The reason all of the checks need to be made out to him is so that the trust fund cannot be sued and all assets taken to pay my expenses. The trust cannot be touched until he is ready for college," explained Doug in a rather shaky voice.

The little boy returned with the refreshments and the conversation took upon itself a lighter tone. Of course, the set was purchased and another large check was made out to the boy to be deposited in the trust.

Earl and Gwen never saw either Doug or the boy after that encounter. Not too long after that, they did see Doug's obituary in the paper. It seems he had been a CPA in a small firm. There was only one survivor listed in the obituary, a son.

Gwen looked at Earl and said, "What it does not say is that he survived by a son who was much loved."

"And a son," said Earl with a light smile, "Who will one day have a college education."

Blood on the Arrowhead

A majority of customers wandering through the antiques show are fascinated by arrowheads. Inherent within them are untold stories about another time and another way of life. The arrowhead in focus was larger than most. Someone had arduously carved housing for it out of a walnut plaque and the arrowhead perfectly fit into the carved hollow. It was the unusual coloration of the stone which caused collectors to look twice. They did not easily recognize what sort of rock would have those dark, rich colors. Little did they know that the color did not come from the rock formation, but was actually the blood of Albert Ambrose Straton.

Albert Ambrose and his wife Maude had acquired a

modest acreage in the woods of central Texas in the 1830's. There they built a two room log cabin and cultivated a three acre garden. However, their chief income came from the hides and furs of small animals which Albert Ambrose trapped. Three children blessed their union and they were relatively content and satisfied with their circumstances. Occasionally one of their neighbors would have some flair up with either the Kiowa or Comanche, but nothing long lasting or too serious.

In the late 1830's, the marauding Comanche became interested in capturing white women and children. The children were trained as slaves and your imagination can conjure up the fate of the women, who were considered quite a prize. Thus it was that the Comanche became aware of the settlement of the Stratons. For several days the raiding party of five braves watched the habits of the frontier family, and when Albert Ambrose left on one of his trapping expeditions, they began to make their move.

Maude and the children spotted them from quite some distance away and realized danger was imminent. She instructed her oldest son, Tom, who was nine at the time, to take the milk cow into the woods and hide the cow in a makeshift shelter they had earlier prepared. No possession was of more value to them than the milk cow. She provided fresh milk daily which was a rarity on the frontier. Regardless of what the Indians intended, if the savages eyed the cow, the animal would be confiscated and eaten. Such a loss would have been tragic to the Stratons.

"Now, Tom," his mother's voice quivered as she spoke, "I know you are a boy, but a man's job has to be done and there is no one else but you to do it." Tom was terrified.

"What if I never see you again?" Tom sobbed.

"Well, at least you will have plenty of milk," his mother tried to joke. However, both Tom and his mother were scared, and the joke fell flat. After an affectionate hug and pat on the head, Tom began the arduous task of leading the cow to their hiding place.

Maude had no gun because Albert Ambrose had both the rifle and the pistol with him. Maude knew that the cabin was impenetrable due to its heavy construction and all openings and doors were bolted from the inside with sturdy planks.

"If I ever get out of this, I'm going back to civilization," vowed Maude under her breath. "No man or land is worth this!" She knew she did not mean the vow but it seemed to give her courage at the moment.

It was not long before the siege, such as it was, began. The Indians banged on the doors and screamed and yelled, pulling all sorts of antics and frightening dances. They threw things around and shouted what Maude believed to be obscenities toward the cabin. No words could describe the fear and anguish in Maude's heart.

The Comanche withdrew when their efforts and antics failed. Maude thought maybe they had given up, but the adrenaline choked her when she heard them on the roof. Immediately she glanced at the stone fireplace and realized that it was large enough for a man to descend if he struggled a bit. Grabbing the mattress off the bed, she and the two younger children stuffed it into the chimney. She sensed that two of the culprits were coming down the chimney and that one of them was stuck. As they got closer to the room, she set fire to the mattress by throwing coal oil on it and seeing it flame away.

No screams or yells were ever fiercer than when the flames began to lick the heels of the Comanche. What clothing they were wearing caught fire and they were severely burned. The one that was stuck got unstuck with miraculous speed and their retreat began.

Albert Ambrose may have heard some commotion or a sixth sense may have called him home. In any case, he returned and was horrified to surmise the situation. Stealthily, he made his way to the storm cellar they had dug near the house and silently raised the door and crawled into the shelter. The door provided him with a perfect cover and his marksmanship was rewarded. One of the Indians was killed and another one was shot in the leg. Maude and Albert Ambrose were never bothered by the Comanche again.

The raiding party retreated, taking their dead, wounded and badly burned ilk with them, but not before launching an arrow into Albert Ambrose's upper right shoulder. Maude eyed him through a peephole crawling toward the house and had the door open. She winced to see the arrow protruding from his back in his shoulder.

Maude and the children somehow got him to the kitchen table. They both knew the arrow had to come out. Too many dangers threatened going to a neighbor's for help or traveling the many miles for a doctor. He was losing so much blood that Maude doubted if he could have made a long trip in the wagon. The arrow refused to budge when pulled backward. To have forced it that way would have made shreds of his shoulder. The arrow had to be pushed all the way through.

Maude was afraid that if she used a small hammer she might miss the arrow and injure her husband even more. Perusing the possibilities, she picked up the heavy black iron skillet, and slammed the butt of the arrow with all her might. She could hear the bone being chipped as the arrow protruded from his front shoulder. Albert Ambrose passed out and fell against the table.

Maude was glad he was unconscious because what she had to do next would be painful. For a moment, she thought about passing out herself. She broke the feathered tail off the arrow. With some tongs grasping the arrowhead, she yanked the piercing weapon free from his body. Managing somehow to get him to the bed while he was still unconscious, she poured whiskey in the opening to sterilize the wound. Then, using an old frontier remedy, she packed the wound with coal oil soaked rags to slow the bleeding. Thankfully, Albert Ambrose slept for several hours.

By nightfall, Tom returned with the milk cow. Albert Ambrose regained consciousness but was in a weakened condition. He was a long time in reclaiming his strength and was never really able to use his right arm and shoulder much again. However, during his convalescence, he carved the little holder for the arrowhead. They hung it on the wall and to this day, if one holds it just right in the light, can be seen the faded inscription underneath the arrowhead:

"Watch … for you know not when the hour cometh."

This was just to remind them of the preciousness and precariousness of life.

Author's Afterglow

On a cold, wintry afternoon in Tulsa very few patrons came to the opening of the antiques show. One old woman, who looked as if she were homeless, wandered in wearing tennis shoes years before they were fashionable and with a stocking cap pulled down over her head. Surprised that she had the price of admission, I supposed she had come in to stay warm for the afternoon. For some reason, she reminded me of how my grandmother would dress when she went out to the barn to gather eggs in the middle of the winter.

The old lady had a nice smile and a good sense of humor and stayed in my booth for a long time. We discussed several of my finest items and she said she would like to make a note of them. All I could find to write upon was a paper napkin, and she made some notes.

"These girandoles with all this colored glass fruit would make you think you were having a party all the time," she stated. "However, as much as they are, there wouldn't be any money left for booze and food to party with."

"Well, to live in a state of partying is priceless," I said and we both laughed.

She next studied an oil painting of a barnyard scene featuring a donkey and some chickens. "The only reason I would buy that is because it reminds me of my husband's family. One more donkey and an old bossy cow would make this their family portrait."

"Well, just think how grateful it would be every time you looked at it and realized they were not visiting you," I teased.

This discussion about my merchandise went on for quite some time. Occasionally she would ask for the best price or make a note on the napkin. I knew we were just playing games, but that was all right because I had nothing better to do. All in all, it was a very pleasant visit. She spent the rest of the afternoon going from booth to booth.

On Sunday afternoon shortly before the show closed, the same old lady in the same old clothes came back into my booth. We greeted one another and she handed me the same old paper napkin and said, "I want these things."

Not quite grasping the situation, I smiled and replied, "Don't we all? I often wish I could afford to take some of them home with me." She gave me a warm little smile and pulled a handful of hundred dollar bills from her pocket.

"I want to buy all of these items on this napkin. They will upgrade my antiques shop mightily." And with that she counted out almost five thousand dollars. As I helped her to carry out several boxes, she said, "You know, you are the only dealer here who made me feel welcome in their booth. Thank you for being so nice."

I learned a valuable lesson that afternoon which was to influence my relationship with the customers for many years. Now I know what the saying means that proclaims: "Never judge a book by its cover."

For over twenty years I had the privilege of getting acquainted with many marvelous individuals. Doing three or four shows a year in the same town every year, (usually the same people attend every show) genuine and abiding friendships developed. I always had a good time at the shows. One favorite customer in New Orleans was an older gentleman who collected expensive Vienna bronze figures. One day he asked, "Do you know what I enjoy most about my collecting?" Of course, I did not know and he explained, "What gives me the most pleasure is thinking about how hard my children are going to have to work to sell all these figures to collect their inheritance."

There was the customer who related the horrifying tale of being in crowded Grand Central Station before WWI. A young lady with a long hatpin turned her head quickly at just the right moment and position catching her hatpin in his ear lobe. Being very polite, he did not yell at her but instead tried to catch her arm. She thought he was trying to accost her and evidently quite a scene ensued. Can you imagine the chaos? Now there is drama personified.

Then there was the friendly patron who had come back to the booth for the third time to consider the elaborate cut glass bowl. When the customer comes back to the booth for the third time, the dealer can usually get one hand on the sales pad. I had cleared a table and put the bowl on a mirrored plateau, making sure it was under a good light. I secured a chair for her to sit on and contemplate how the bowl would grace her dining table, but all of a sudden she jumped up and said, "I can't buy this bowl. It just reminds me too much of my second husband."

Now a wise man would have left that alone, but not me, so I had to ask how that bowl was like her second husband. She candidly told me, "I had absolutely no use nor need for him, but did I have the "hots" to take him home with me." Perhaps the fact that I burst out laughing contributed to my loss of the sale.

A regular patron who almost always bought generously from me was accompanied to the show by her husband. I was very fond of them but did grimace a little when I heard him say within my hearing, "Oh, hell. Turner's here and this is going to cost us."

I still cringe when I remember the wealthy young matron who purchased a beautiful Baccarat cut glass centerpiece mounted in gold plated bronze. It was one of my most artistic pieces and I had envisioned it in an elaborate table setting. As I took her check for $4600, I asked how she planned to use it. Her reply was, "I thought it would make a nice soap dish for my guest bathroom." I had the same emotional reaction when a woman bought a gorgeous sterling silver ferner to use as a water dish for her poodle.

I first heard the story of the overturned outhouse when I was a little boy at a family reunion. My father and his uncle, who were the same age, finally admitted that they had been the ones who tickled their mothers' behinds with the twigs, causing the two women to jump up and entrap themselves in the privy. Now that incident had occurred over thirty years before that reunion, yet my grandmother and her sister, who were the victims in the prank, got so angry at the confession that it almost ruined the family reunion.

Those two boys were also the ones who exchanged the babies in the wagons. My great grandfather, who was a circuit rider preacher, was the one who preached with a gun on the side of his pulpit. Having often heard the story of the woman burning the mattress and the boy hiding the cow from the Indians from my paternal grandmother, I believe that it is an account of my great, great grandparents.

My maternal grandmother was one of the little girls who got thrown off the train. The story of the cranberry glasses is an account of her wedding day. That family was to give the land for Henslee Chapel where the Squirrel Stew Supper took place and the recipe is from the Henslee Family Cookbook.

Perhaps my moment of greatest chagrin occurred at a show in Texas. At the preceding show I had taken in some bad checks and three bad credit cards. I was anxious that it not happen again and vowed to deal only with respectable people. There was a circus on the same grounds as the antiques show. In the middle of the afternoon two women, who were perfect stereotypes of hookers, came into the booth. The woman who carried a very large bag began to pick up items and place them over on the place where I wrapped sold items. She accrued quite a pile.

Now I was thinking about how I was going to handle the situation because there was no way that I was going to take checks from those two. Stalling for time, I tactlessly asked, "What do you ladies do for a living?" Regretting the words before they even got out of my mouth, they responded with an icy look in their eyes that they were with the circus. "Isn't that wonderful," I thought cynically.

My mind raced as to how to tell these two painted ladies that I was neither going to take their checks nor their credit cards. Careful not to insult them by refusing their business and thereby creating a scene, I stalled for time to think, "And what do you do with the circus?"

Reading my thoughts exactly, the woman with the large bag pulled it open to reveal more cash than I had ever seen in my entire life. Smiling sweetly and knowingly, she replied, "I own the circus!" Well, that was a sale that made my show, as well as teaching me a valuable lesson.

Almost all of the stories are based on actual events. I have taken the liberty of presenting them to you as fictional and have colored them up a bit. My purpose is to help us remember lifestyles long past and the price that has been paid for us to be here and to say "Thank You" to the Past. I do hope that you have been pleasured by these tales as much as I have enjoyed sharing them with you.